For Elizabeth and Terri

Copyright © 2000 by Mary Morgan Van Royen.
All rights reserved. No part of this book may be reproduced or transmitted in any form or
by any means, electronic or mechanical, including photocopying, recording, or by any information storage
and retrieval system, without written permission from the publisher. For information address
Hyperion Books for Children, 114 Fifth Avenue, New York, New York 10011-5690.
This book is set in 30 pt. Kennerley
First Edition
1 3 5 7 9 10 8 6 4 2

Printed in Singapore.

Library of Congress Cataloging-in-Publication Data
Morgan-Vanroyen, Mary, 1957-
Patient Rosie/Mary Morgan—1st ed.
p. cm.
Summary: A little mouse waits patiently while her fur is combed, until it is her turn, for cookies to cool
before eating them, and for her seeds to grow.
ISBN 0-7868-0476-9 (trade)
[1. Mice—Fiction. 2. Patience—Fiction.] I. Title.
PZ7.V353Pat 2000
[E]—dc21 99-20982

Visit www.hyperionchildrensbooks.com,
part of the GO Network

To Rosie... Happy 2 Birthday... Love Aunt Jill

Patient ROSIE

MARY MORGAN

HYPERION BOOKS FOR CHILDREN

NEW YORK

Rosie is patient.

She sits very still while Mama combs her fur.

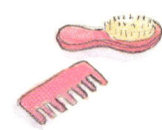

Rosie waits her turn.

She lets the cookies cool before eating one.

Rosie hangs her paintings
only when they're all dry.

She watches for the rain to stop, so she can go out and play.

Rosie waits . . .
and waits . . .
for her seeds to grow.

Now Rosie has
beautiful flowers!
What a patient mouse.